Ladybird Readers

Jazz the Vet

Series Editor: Sorrel Pitts
Story by Catherine Baker

Ladybird Readers Starter Level

	Title	Phonics	Sight Words
1	Alphabet Book	A—Z	
2	Is it Nat?	s a t p i n	a is it
3	Nat Sits		an in sit
4	Top Dog and Pompom	m d g o c k	and can I into no
5	Top Dog is Sick		got not
6	The Fun Run	e u r h b f l	at get go has off the to up
7	Gus is Hot!		full his of on put
8	Jazz the Vet	j v w x y z qu	be but had he him she tell was
9	Vick the Vet		did well will
10	Dash and Thud	ch sh th ng	if ran then they with yes
11	Big Bad Bash		big long that this
12	The Big Fish	ai ee oa oo	her look see them
13	The Big Ship		let me my too
14	Martin and Lorna	ar or ur ow oi er	all are for
15	Farmer Carl		cut down good help now
16	The Big Dipper	igh ear air ure	as have like said some went you
17	The Silver Ring		come from so stop we what

First, go through the phonemes on page 4, and do the activity on page 5. Then, read the words in the first half of the book, focusing on pronunciation and blending.

The sight words are introduced in the second half of the book, first on their own and then in full sentences.

At the back of the book, there are activities and assessments practicing phonemes and sight words. These icons indicate the key skills required in each activity:

 Spelling and writing   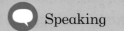 Speaking   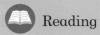 Reading

Ladybird Readers

Jazz the Vet

Look at the story

First, look at the words and pictures.
Use the words to practice phonics.

Phonics focus

Jazz   vet   Zac

fix   jab   yell

Wendy   quick   six

Aa Bb Cc Dd Ee Ff Gg Hh Ii Jj Kk Ll Mm

Activity

1 **Say the first sound. Match.**

Jazz   Wendy   quick

j   z   w   qu

jab   Zac

Zac

6

Jazz

vet

Jazz

fix   jab

Wendy

yell

Jazz

quick

jab

Jazz

six

Jazz the Vet

Read the story

Now read the story in full sentences.
Practice using the sight words.

Sight words

be

but

had

he

him

she

tell

was

Zac and his dad visit Jazz the vet.

Zac's rabbit has a bad leg.

Jazz picks up the rabbit and rubs its leg.

Jazz tells Zac he can fix
the leg. The rabbit gets a jab
in the top of its leg.

Wendy visits the vet. She has a big, red parrot. The parrot yells at Jazz.

Jazz has to be quick.
The parrot will nip him.

A man has a big bag.
He unzips the bag.
It has seven kittens in it!

The kittens get jabs.
Jazz gives the man
a tub of pills.

Jazz has to put the kittens back into the bag. He has six kittens, not seven!

A kitten was in a big box.
She had a nap!

Activities

2 Say the sounds. Circle the words with the same sound.

1   z   fix   (Zac)   quick

2   x   six   Wendy   jab

3   qu   Jazz   vet   quick

4   j   jab   six   vet

5   y   Zac   yell   kittens

3 Match the sight words.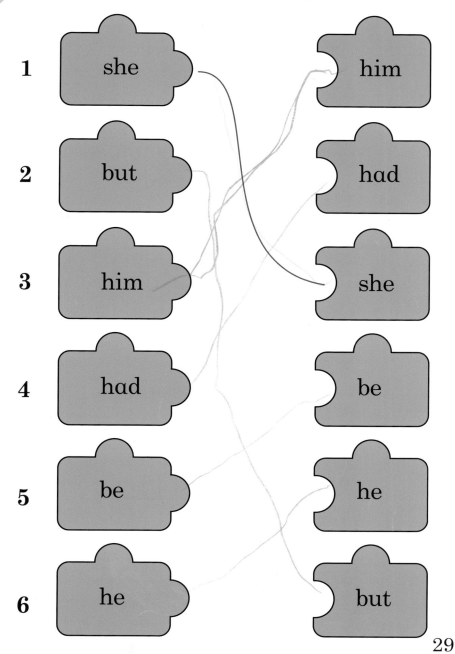

1	she	him
2	but	had
3	him	she
4	had	be
5	be	he
6	he	but

29

Assessment

4 **Look. Write the correct letters. Say the words.**

(J) (v) (W) (x) (y) (Z) (qu)

1 **W**endy's parrot **y**ells.

2 ___azz is a ___et.

3 There are si___ kittens.

4 Jazz has to be ___ick.

5 ___ac visits the vet.

5 Choose the correct words, and write them on the lines.

be   had   he

tells   was

1   Jazz tells Zac he can fix the leg.

2   She _____ a nap!

3   Jazz has to _____ quick!

4   A kitten _____ in a big box.

Starter

Alphabet Book Starter 1	**Is it Nat?** Starter 2	**Nat Sits** Starter 3	**Top Dog and Pompom** Starter 4	**Top Dog is Sick** Starter 5
978-0-241-39367-3	978-0-241-39368-0	978-0-241-39369-7	978-0-241-39370-3	978-0-241-39371-0
The Fun Run Starter 6	**Gus is Hot!** Starter 7	**Jazz the Vet** Starter 8	**Vick the Vet** Starter 9	**Dash and Thud** Starter 10
978-0-241-39372-7	978-0-241-39373-4	978-0-241-39374-1	978-0-241-39375-8	978-0-241-39376-5
Big Bad Bash Starter 11	**The Big Fish** Starter 12	**The Big Ship** Starter 13	**Martin and Lorna** Starter 14	**Farmer Carl** Starter 15
978-0-241-39377-2	978-0-241-39379-6	978-0-241-39380-2	978-0-241-39381-9	978-0-241-39382-6
The Big Dipper Starter 16	**The Silver Ring** Starter 17			
978-0-241-39383-3	978-0-241-39384-0			

LADYBIRD BOOKS

UK | USA | Canada | Ireland | Australia
India | New Zealand | South Africa

Ladybird Books is part of the Penguin Random House group of companies
whose addresses can be found at global.penguinrandomhouse.com.
www.penguin.co.uk   www.puffin.co.uk   www.ladybird.co.uk

Penguin
Random House
UK

First published 2017. This edition published 2019
001

Copyright © Ladybird Books Ltd, 2017

Printed in China

A CIP catalogue record for this book is available from the British Library

ISBN: 978-0-241-39374-1

All correspondence to:
Ladybird Books
Penguin Random House Children's
80 Strand, London WC2R 0RL